Angels Don't Know Karate

There are more books about the Bailey School Kids!
Have you read these adventures?

Angels Don't Know Karate

by Debbie Dadey
and
Marcia Thornton Jones

illustrated by John Steven Gurney

———
A
LITTLE APPLE
PAPERBACK
———

SCHOLASTIC INC.
New York Toronto London Auckland Sydney

No part of this publication may be reproduced in whole or in part, or stored in a retrieval system, or transmitted in any form or by any means, electronic, mechanical, photocopying, recording, or otherwise, without written permission of the publisher. For information regarding permission, write to Scholastic Inc., 555 Broadway, New York, NY 10012.

ISBN 0-590-84902-6

22 21 20 19 18   1/0

Printed in the U.S.A.   40

First Scholastic printing, November 1996

Book design by Laurie Williams

To Jared Thornton, Allison Thornton,
Nathan Dadey, and Rebekah Dadey —
four very special angels!
—MTJ and DD

Contents

Angels Don't Know Karate

1

Angels, Angels, Everywhere

Melody fell back on the ground and waved her arms and legs in big arcs. When she jumped up, there was a perfect angel in the snow. "Watch out," she hollered to her friend Eddie. "You almost trampled one of my angels."

It was a few weeks before Christmas. Melody and Eddie and their friends Liza and Howie were on the Bailey School playground playing in the fluffy snow. Other kids had built a snowman and Eddie was in the middle of bombarding them with snowballs packed extra hard.

"How do you expect us to have a decent snowball fight?" Eddie grumbled. "There are angels everywhere."

Melody smiled. "Of course there are.

We all have guardian angels. That's what my mother told me when she gave me this." She pointed to the little gold pin on her coat's collar.

Howie laughed. "Everybody but Eddie," he said. "No angel would come near Eddie!"

"You better hope your guardian angel is paying attention," Eddie warned, "because you're about to get creamed with this snowball." Eddie took aim and let the snowball fly.

"Duck!" Liza screamed. But Howie didn't move fast enough. The snowball smacked him right in the chest.

"Howie's angel must have gone home for Christmas," Eddie said.

Melody grabbed Eddie's arm before he could throw another snowball. "Don't you believe in angels?" she asked.

"Everybody has a guardian angel," Liza said. "Even you."

"Then I hope that new crossing guard

has one," Eddie said. He jerked his arm away from Melody and pointed to the street.

A stranger wearing a bright white cape and gold earmuffs was bending over in the middle of the street. Near her was a bright orange sign that read CROSSING GUARD. With a fat paintbrush, she was re-painting the faded crosswalk stripes.

"She better be careful," Liza said. "A car could run over her."

Eddie agreed. "She'd be flatter than a dime on a railroad track."

"She needs a guardian angel," Melody said as the stranger set her can of paint down on the sidewalk across the street. "If she spills paint on mean Mr. Mason's sidewalk she'll be a goner."

The kids stared at Mr. Mason's yard. It was the only one around without any Christmas decorations. Everybody knew about mean Mr. Mason. It was said he cooked kids in his stew if he found them in his yard.

"Maybe somebody should warn that stranger before Mr. Mason catches her," Liza said.

Eddie opened his mouth to speak, but before he had the chance a snowball bopped him right in the mouth. "Ow!" Eddie screamed.

"A direct hit!" a boy named Ben yelled loud enough for everyone in the school

5

yard to hear. Ben was in the fourth grade and liked to bully third-graders. Especially Eddie.

Eddie grabbed a handful of snow to throw at Ben. "I'm not going to let him get away with that," Eddie said. "I wish I knew karate. I'd sidekick him all the way to Sheldon City."

"Don't worry about it," Howie said. "It was only snow."

"Eddie's chicken," Ben yelled and flapped his arms. "Bok! Bok! Bok!"

"I'm not chicken," Eddie blurted. "I'm not afraid of anything."

"Yes, you are," Ben shouted. "You're afraid of a little snowball fight. I bet you're even afraid of climbing trees."

"Am not," Eddie sputtered.

Ben walked up close to Eddie until their noses almost touched. "I dare you to prove it. I double dare you!"

Eddie put his hands on his hips. "I'll prove it," he said. "You just wait and see."

2

Double Dare

"Don't do it," Melody said. "It's too dangerous."

Howie nodded. "Especially in this snow. Those branches will be icy."

Eddie held his head up high. "I have to," he said. "Ben double dared me."

"That just means Ben is twice as dumb," Melody said. "And if you climb that tree, you'll be two times dumber than he is!"

Eddie thought about that for a moment. But he wasn't very good at math so he decided to ignore his friend.

"Get out of my way," Eddie said. "I'm going to set the Bailey School record for tree climbing!"

Eddie kicked through the snow until he reached the giant oak tree on the playground. The tree was usually their favorite meeting place, but today it looked like a monster stretching all the way up to the sky.

"Don't do it," Howie warned. "You'll get hurt."

Eddie didn't listen. He grabbed the lowest branch and hoisted himself up. Then he scrambled to the next branch and the next. A small crowd of kids gathered around the trunk and stared as he climbed higher and higher.

"You better stop," Melody called.

"You're too high already," Liza added.

Howie shaded his eyes from the bright winter sun. "The cold will make the branches brittle," he warned. "They'll snap off in your hands!"

Just then, Eddie's boot slipped on the slick bark. He reached for a branch, but it broke off in his hands. Eddie scrambled to stop himself from falling, but it was too late.

Liza screamed and Howie's face turned snow white as their best friend tumbled down from branch to branch.

"Look!" Melody gasped. "The branches aren't breaking!"

It was true. The frozen branches handed Eddie down from tree limb to tree limb. When there were no more branches Liza closed her eyes. She didn't want to see her friend crash to the ground. Only, Eddie didn't fall. He landed right in the out-stretched arms of the new crossing guard.

The kids on the playground cheered, but Melody grabbed Howie's and Liza's arms. "Did you see that?" Melody whispered to Howie.

"Of course I did," Howie told her. "We all saw Eddie fall."

Melody shook her head. "I don't mean that."

"What are you talking about?" Liza asked.

"The stranger. When she reached up to

catch Eddie, it looked like she had wings," Melody said. Then she whispered, "Angel wings."

Melody's last words were drowned out by cheers for the stranger. Howie and Liza rushed over to check on Eddie. The stranger gently set him on the ground.

"Oh, Eddie," Liza said. "I'm so glad you're all right."

Howie patted Eddie on the shoulder. "You could have been killed."

"Thank goodness you saved him," Liza told the stranger.

Melody came up behind Liza. "Where did you come from anyway?" Melody asked.

The stranger smiled and pointed upward to the sky over the street.

"We saw you painting the street," Eddie said. "You must have practically flown over here to catch me."

"No," Melody said firmly. "I mean, where did you *really* come from?"

"Oh," the stranger said. "I'm new in town. I just dropped in for the holidays." The stranger's voice was soft and musical sounding.

"Are you visiting family?" Liza asked.

"No," the stranger said. "I'm here for the opening of a new karate school. There will be a karate demonstration at the mall this afternoon. Perhaps you'd like coupons for a free lesson next week."

"All right!" Eddie yelled. "That's what I just wished for!"

The stranger smiled. "Karate is much safer than climbing frozen trees!"

"Thank you for the coupons," Liza said. "And for saving Eddie's life. I'm Liza and these are my friends Howie and Melody."

The stranger smiled and put her hand on Liza's shoulder. "It is delightful to meet you. My name is Angela Michaels. I know I will be seeing you again soon. Farewell for now."

Liza watched the stranger walk away.

She walked so smoothly, she seemed to glide over the snow. "That woman is so nice," Liza said.

"Pretty, too," Howie said, blushing.

Eddie had to agree. "I guess for once, I was lucky. I'd probably be in the hospital if it wasn't for her."

"It wasn't luck," Melody said to herself. "It was a miracle."

3

The Mall

"Hurry up!" Eddie said. "I want to get a good seat to watch someone get karate chopped!"

"Sounds good to me," Melody yelled. "Last one there is a frozen booger."

The kids raced up Smith Avenue to the mall. Garlands full of twinkling colored lights crisscrossed the mall entrance. Melody pointed toward a huge crowd gathered near a giant Christmas tree. "I guess the karate demonstration has started."

"Neat," Eddie said, doing a karate chop in the air. "Let's go see someone get their head knocked off."

"That's disgusting," Liza said. "I don't want to watch that."

"Karate isn't really like that," Howie told them. "It isn't about hurting people. It's more about protecting and . . ."

"Guarding," Melody added.

"Right," Howie said. "It's also good exercise. I might even get to take lessons if it isn't too expensive."

"That's enough talk," Eddie said. "Let's go see some action!" Eddie led the way into the crowd. In three short minutes, Eddie had wiggled his way to the front of the huge group of people, with Liza, Melody, and Howie right behind him.

"Watch this," Howie whispered. "Someone is going to break that stack of wood with their bare hands."

"No way," Liza said. "I couldn't even do that with a hammer."

The karate expert stood with her head down. Her long blond hair was wound into a bun on top of her head and tied with a gold ribbon. She was barefoot and

dressed in white, except for the black belt wrapped around her waist.

"I think she's checking to make sure her toenails are clean." Eddie giggled.

"Shhh," Howie said. "She's concentrating."

"Kee-YAW!" the karate expert screamed, and slammed her hand into the wood.

Liza and Eddie jumped. Melody almost fell into the crowd. "That's the loudest concentrating I've ever heard," Eddie said.

"Look," Howie said. "She did it."

The entire stack of wood was broken neatly in two. Everyone clapped. The expert turned around and yelled again. "Kee-YAW!" This time she broke another stack of wood with her bare foot.

"Ouch," Eddie said. "That had to hurt."

Howie and Liza nodded. Melody just stood staring at the karate expert.

"Oh, my gosh," Melody said. "Look who it is!"

4

Mr. Mason

"Angela Michaels is the best karate expert ever," Eddie told his friends on their way to school on Monday. "Kee-YAW!" Eddie yelled, kicking a little snow with his boot.

"Watch it, kid!" shouted Mr. Mason from his porch. "I just shoveled that sidewalk!"

"Sorry," Liza said quickly, grabbing Eddie's arm and pulling him toward the school.

"I wasn't hurting his sidewalk," Eddie grumbled when they got to the crosswalk. "He's just an old grump."

"He's so mean Santa Claus probably doesn't even visit him," Melody said.

"Mr. Mason scares me," Liza told them. "He practically bit Eddie's head off just for kicking a little snow."

"A tadpole would scare you," Eddie snickered. "Maybe Mr. Mason needs Angela Michaels to give him a couple of karate chops."

"Maybe she could knock some sense into him," Liza said.

"He sure needs something," Melody agreed.

"There she is," Liza said. "Why don't you ask her?" Liza pointed to the middle of the street. Angela Michaels stood in the crosswalk blowing a whistle. She was wearing gold earmuffs, white boots, white jeans, and a long white cape.

A red car drove slowly up Delaware Boulevard toward the crosswalk. Angela Michaels raised her arms and blew her whistle so hard Liza had to cover her ears. The car slammed on its brakes and came to a dead stop.

Angela Michaels motioned for the kids to cross the street. Eddie, Liza, and Howie walked into the crosswalk, but Melody stared at Angela Michaels.

"Come on," Liza said, pulling Melody's arm.

"What's wrong with you?" Howie asked after they'd crossed the street. "You look like you've seen a ghost."

"Close," Melody told him. "Only this

isn't the kind that haunts people. This is the kind that protects them."

"What are you talking about?" Eddie asked.

"I'm talking about angels," Melody said. "Guardian angels!"

5

Angel with a Mission

Eddie looked over at the playground, but Melody's snow angels had been trampled long ago. Not a single one was left. "I guess it's too bad your angels are smooshed, but it's nothing to get upset about."

"I'm not talking about snow angels," Melody said.

Liza patted her friend on the back. "Then what in the world are you talking about?"

"Nothing in *this* world," Melody said. She pointed to a fluffy cloud floating overhead. "I'm talking about something from up there!"

Melody led her friends away from the street and behind a giant snowman. Then

she whispered, "I believe Angela Michaels is an angel," she said. "A guardian angel!"

Howie's eyes got big and Liza gasped. But Eddie laughed so hard he fell down in the snow.

"First you saw angels in the snow," Eddie said once he caught his breath. "Now, you're seeing them in the middle of the street! Next, you'll be seeing them in the school cafeteria!"

"Eddie's right," Howie told Melody. "Angels aren't crossing guards."

"Angels fly around working miracles," Eddie added.

"And they definitely don't know karate," Liza said.

Melody nodded. "They protect people. That's what Miss Michaels did when Eddie fell from the tree. She also gave Eddie his wish."

"What wish?" Eddie said.

"Don't you remember?" Melody said.

"You wished to know karate. And now you have a coupon for a free karate lesson."

Howie kicked at a frozen lump of snow. "It did seem like a miracle when those branches kept Eddie from crashing to the ground."

"That was no miracle," Eddie told them. "It was luck."

"Maybe that's what miracles are," Liza said softly.

Melody nodded so hard her hat fell off and plopped into a puddle of slush. "Most people call it luck. But not me. I believe they're miracles. Our guardian angels make them happen. And right now, our angel is directing traffic!"

Eddie snorted and Liza giggled. Even Howie smiled. "Why would an angel come to Bailey City?" he asked Melody.

"Bailey City is the perfect place for angels," Melody said.

"Not with Eddie around." Liza giggled. "That's enough to scare away any angel."

Eddie held up his hand to karate chop Liza's arm, but Melody stopped him. "Even with Eddie," Melody argued, "Bailey City is full of nice people."

"But why would an angel choose to visit us now?" Howie asked.

"Maybe," Melody said slowly, "she's an angel with a mission."

6

Spying on an Angel

"The only mission an angel would have is to knock sense into your head." Eddie laughed. Then he pretended to karate chop the air in front of Melody's nose.

"Laugh all you want," Melody warned. "But I'm going to prove Angela Michaels is an angel."

Then Melody tromped through the snow to the doors of Bailey Elementary. That afternoon when school was over, she didn't wait for her friends.

"Where are you going?" Liza yelled.

"To talk to an angel," Melody called over her shoulder.

Liza, Howie, and Eddie hurried to catch up with Melody. "You can't just walk up to the new crossing guard and ask if she's an angel," Howie said.

"She'll think you're crazy," Eddie added. "Of course, if she's really an angel, she'd already know that."

Melody glared at Eddie. "You're right. I don't have proof. Maybe if we spy on her, you'll see that Miss Michaels is no ordinary crossing guard."

"Spying?" Eddie interrupted. "Now you're talking. Spying is my specialty. Follow me!"

Eddie sneaked behind a row of bushes. He paused to make sure his three friends were close behind, then he darted from tree to tree until he was at a corner far down the street.

"We can't even see Miss Michaels from here," Melody snapped. "What kind of spy are you?"

"The best kind," Eddie said with a grin. "Sneaky. Just follow me and you'll see." He looked both ways to check for traffic before quickly crossing the street. He led them around a block and through three backyards. Finally, he stopped.

"That," he said, pointing between a gap in a long row of bushes, "is the perfect place for spying on Melody's angel."

Liza gasped and Howie's eyes got big. Melody swallowed hard. When she spoke, her voice trembled. "Are you out of your mind?"

"You wanted to spy on Miss Michaels, didn't you?" Eddie asked.

Melody nodded. "Yes, but —"

"And you don't want to be caught, do you?" Eddie interrupted.

Melody shook her head. "No, but —"

"Then this is the perfect spying spot," Eddie said. "No one would ever expect to find kids hiding in mean Mr. Mason's yard."

"That's because no kids are dumb enough to go there," Liza blurted.

"Except us," Eddie said proudly. "And I thought of it!"

"That makes you dumber than everyone!" Howie told him.

Eddie thought about that for a split second. Then his face got red and he rolled his fingers into a fist. "Are you calling me dumb?" he snapped.

"No," Melody said quickly before her two friends started a fight. "He's just saying that we shouldn't go there." She looked into Mr. Mason's backyard. "It's not safe. Everybody knows it."

"But if Miss Michaels is really a guardian angel," Eddie said, "we have nothing to worry about. Right?" He looked Melody straight in the eyes. "Or don't you believe in angels anymore?"

"I believe," Melody said, "that guardian angels help us make safe decisions. Going in there is *not* safe."

"You're just chicken," Eddie told her. He hooked his thumbs under his arms and flapped them like a big chicken.

"Of course, she's chicken," Howie said.

"Everyone's afraid to go near Mr. Mason. If he caught us in his yard he'd cook us for dinner and no one would ever know what happened to us."

"Then we won't get caught," Eddie said. "Now, let's go." Eddie slipped through the gap in the bushes before his friends could stop him.

"We can't let him go alone," Liza whispered.

"Sure, we can," Howie said.

"But what if he needs our help?" Melody asked. "We're his friends." Melody didn't wait for them to answer before disappearing through the bushes.

Liza looked at Howie and Howie looked at Liza. "I have a feeling I'm going to regret this," Liza said. Then she and Howie followed their friends into mean Mr. Mason's backyard.

7

Perfect Job for an Angel

Howie and Liza tiptoed across Mr. Mason's backyard. They stooped low when they went by a window. They found Eddie and Melody crouched under the giant evergreen tree in the front yard.

They peeked around the low hanging branches and watched Miss Michaels blow her whistle to stop traffic.

"She's the prettiest crossing guard Bailey City ever had," Howie whispered.

"She has golden curls," Melody said, "just like an angel should."

"But she's not an angel," Eddie said. "I told you, angels aren't crossing guards."

"Crossing *guard* is a perfect job for a *guard*ian angel," Melody said. "She even has a golden halo."

"Those are just earmuffs," Eddie said.

They watched Miss Michaels hold up her arms while a group of first-graders walked across the street.

"Don't you see her wings?" Melody asked.

"That's only a baggy cape," Howie told her.

"Or maybe," Melody said, "her coat sleeves have to be extra big to fit her angel wings!"

"Maybe she just has lots of muscles from breaking stacks of wood," Eddie said. He karate chopped an evergreen branch near his head, but it didn't break.

"She should karate chop your thick skull," Melody snapped.

"Shh," Liza warned. "We're not supposed to be fighting. We're supposed to be spying."

"I'm not sure why we're spying," Howie said. "I don't think Miss Michaels is going to sprout wings and fly up to a cloud right in front of our eyes."

Just then a voice as harsh as sandpaper sent goose bumps racing up their necks. "What are you doing on my property?"

Liza screamed and Howie grabbed Melody's arm. Eddie fell down in the snow and pulled his coat up over his head.

"Answer me!" the rough voice snapped.

The four kids looked into the mean gray eyes of Mr. Mason and gulped.

8

Mr. Mason's Dinner

Mr. Mason pushed his cap back and squinted at the kids. His gray eyebrows came together in a bushy arch. He stuck his wrinkled face down close to the branches.

"This is it!" Liza squealed and hid behind Melody.

"We're going to be the meatballs for Mr. Mason's spaghetti!" Eddie said.

"What kind of trouble are you up to in my yard?" Mr. Mason shouted.

"W — we're sorry," Howie stuttered. "We didn't hurt your yard."

Mr. Mason grabbed Howie by the coat collar and pulled him out from beneath the branches. "I have half a mind to call the police," Mr. Mason growled.

"I doubt that will be necessary," said a sweet voice. It was Angela Michaels. She had her hand on Mr. Mason's arm. "The children were just playing. There is no harm done. Let me fix you a cup of Heavenly Tea," Miss Michaels said, gently leading him inside his front door. "I'm sure you'll feel better."

"Let's get out of here!" Eddie hollered. The four kids scrambled out from the bushes and raced down the street. They didn't stop until they were at the next corner under the streetlight.

"I thought we were goners," Liza panted.

"We would have been if Miss Michaels hadn't saved us," Howie agreed.

Melody put her hands on her hips. "See! I told you she's a guardian angel."

Eddie rolled his eyes. "You're not going to start that baloney again, are you?"

"It's not baloney," Melody said. "She's

an angel with a mission and I've figured out exactly what her mission is."

"What?" Liza asked.

"She wants to help Mr. Mason make friends," Melody told them.

"Are you crazy?" Eddie snapped. "Mr. Mason boils his friends in oil. He makes a terrorist look like Little Red Riding Hood. He's nothing but plain mean!"

"You'd be mean, too, if you didn't have any friends," Melody said softly. "And that's where we come in. We're going to be Mr. Mason's friends!"

"Now you've lost it," Eddie said, shaking his head. "Angela Michaels is not an angel, and you're definitely a kook."

"She is an angel," Melody said firmly. "Didn't you see how Mr. Mason just melted into a big teddy bear around her?"

"Maybe he's in love." Howie laughed.

"Or maybe Miss Michaels has some

special power over people," Melody said.

Liza tapped Melody's arm. "Maybe," Liza suggested, "she has fairy dust like Tinkerbell in *Peter Pan*."

Eddie stomped his foot. "If she has fairy dust, then I'm going to fly away to Never-neverland with the Lost Boys."

"I don't know about magic dust," Melody said. "But I do know that making friends with Mr. Mason is the right thing to do."

"If you're a lunatic," Eddie said with a smirk.

"Then I guess I'm loony," Melody said. "Because I'm going to start right now by taking Mr. Mason some cookies. Then I'm going to shovel his front porch."

"Mr. Mason will turn you into chopped angel toes," Eddie said.

"That's disgusting," Liza told Eddie.

"No," Howie said. "It's disgusting what

Mr. Mason will do to you if he catches you in his yard again."

Melody smiled. "My guardian angel will take care of me. I'm going to be his friend. And if you're my friends, you'll help."

9

Angel Cookies

"It looks as if Huey is the one who needs a friend," Eddie said, motioning across the street. Ben and Huey were both standing in the soccer field. At least Ben was standing. Huey was sitting on the frozen ground, staring up at Ben.

"Is Ben picking on poor Huey?" Liza asked.

"I think Ben is using Huey for karate practice," Howie told them. Ben kicked his foot all around Huey.

"Kee-YAW!" Ben yelled, doing karate chops in the air over Huey's head.

"We better help," Melody said, "before one of those karate chops hurts Huey."

"If we go over there," Eddie told her, "Ben will just use us for target practice.

And I, for one, don't feel like getting broken in two like one of those stacks of wood at the mall."

"We have to do something," Liza said. "After all, he can't chop us all to pieces."

Eddie opened his mouth to argue when the kids saw Ben lift his hand high above Huey's head. Ben's hand came down hard in a karate chop.

"NO!" Liza screamed.

But Ben's hand didn't hit Huey. A white-gloved hand caught Ben's wrist like a steel trap. The white hand lifted Ben off the ground as if he were floating.

"It's Angela Michaels!" Melody said. "She saved Huey."

The kids watched with their mouths hanging open as Miss Michaels held up Ben and talked to him. Her voice drifted across the street and the kids could hear some of her words.

"Karate," she said, "is not for bullying the weaker. The strong among us must

protect the weaker. Do you understand this?"

Ben nodded and Miss Michaels lowered him to the ground. "Now," she said, "go help your friend."

Ben ran over to Huey and helped him off the ground. Ben even dusted the snow off Huey's pants before Huey ran home.

"See?" Melody whispered. "She does have special powers. She *is* an angel and she wants us to make friends. And we're going to start with Mr. Mason!"

"We're not going to do anything with Mr. Mason, yet," Eddie told Melody. He held up a free karate lesson coupon. "First we'll check out Miss Michaels at the karate studio. Then you'll see that she's no angel!"

Melody nodded. "Fine. But then we'll be nice to Mr. Mason."

Eddie shook his head. "That's like being nice to the Abominable Snowman himself. Come on, let's hurry before we lose Miss Michaels."

Melody, Liza, Howie, and Eddie followed Miss Michaels down Delaware Boulevard. They followed her as she turned right onto Main Street and then left onto Forest Lane.

"She's heading for Brewbaker's Dance and Gym Emporium," Liza whispered.

"Either that, or the cemetery," Eddie said.

Melody held her breath when Miss Michaels paused in front of the cemetery and lifted her hand. "I bet she's waving to all her dead friends," Eddie giggled.

"Eddie, stop it," Liza warned. "Maybe angels really do help us."

"All I want Miss Michaels to help me with is karate," Eddie said.

Howie pointed to Brewbaker's Dance and Gym Emporium. "There she is," he said. Miss Michaels was already going in the door. The four kids raced to catch up.

They stopped when they were inside the dark building.

"This place is creepy," Melody said, looking around the gloomy hallway.

"Not that white room," Liza said. The four kids stared at a bright white room off to the side of the dark hallway. A gold band ran around the top of the room and gold mats covered the walls. Gold and blue punching bags hung in one corner. Five figures all dressed in white stood at the far end of the room.

"Oh, my gosh!" Melody squealed. "It's a whole flock of angels!"

10

Ma'am! Yes, Ma'am!

The five figures shouted loudly, "Ma'am! Yes, Ma'am!"

"I thought angels were quiet," Eddie teased. "These obviously flunked peacefulness in heaven."

"They aren't angels," Howie said. "They're Miss Michaels' students."

Miss Michaels stepped out from behind the white-clad students and motioned to Howie, Melody, Liza, and Eddie. "Welcome," she said. "Please take off your shoes and slip on those white uniforms hanging on the wall."

The kids followed directions and bounced over to Miss Michaels. They stood in line facing her.

"Karate," Miss Michaels said, "is full of

discipline. To be an expert, you must have control of your mind and body."

Miss Michaels paused and the five white-clad students yelled, "Ma'am! Yes, Ma'am!"

Eddie giggled. "Are we in the army?"

Miss Michaels looked at Eddie and said. "We will begin with jumping jacks."

"Great," Eddie said.

The four kids had no problem with the

first ten jumping jacks. Or the first twenty. But by number thirty, Liza was barely keeping up and even Eddie was slowing down. By number forty, Melody, Liza, and Howie had stopped and were panting. Eddie was determined not to quit, but when Miss Michaels stopped at fifty he was red-faced. He was too out of breath to even crack a joke.

Miss Michaels smiled and demonstrated a sidekick. Then each student had a chance to practice. Liza fell down and Eddie giggled. Miss Michaels looked at Eddie and said, "Twenty sit-ups. Ready? Begin!"

By the time they had done the sit-ups, the kids were so tired they were sprawled on the floor. Miss Michaels demonstrated a front kick and then called for them to line up again.

"I think I'm dead," Eddie said as he peeled himself off the floor.

Miss Michaels waited until everyone was standing up straight in a line. Then she spoke in her clear musical voice. "Be proud of yourself and remember to watch out for others. Karate is control! Be in control of yourself — not others!" Then Miss Michaels bowed and the white-clad students bowed to her. "Ma'am! Yes, Ma'am!" they yelled.

Eddie, Melody, Liza, and Howie slowly changed back into their clothes. They made their way to the door and put on their shoes and coats.

"I've never been so sore," Liza complained.

"See," Eddie told Melody. "Miss Michaels isn't an angel. She's really an army drill sergeant in disguise."

Melody stood up straight. "Weren't you paying attention? She's an angel and she told us to watch out for others. And we'll start with Mr. Mason!"

11

The Nicest Thing

"This has got to be the stupidest thing we've ever done," Eddie complained the next afternoon. "And we've done some pretty stupid things."

Melody shook her head. "It's the nicest thing we've ever done."

"I'm too sore to be nice," Eddie grumbled.

Eddie, Melody, Howie, and Liza were on their way to Mr. Mason's house. Melody and Howie each carried a plate of homemade Christmas cookies. Eddie and Liza carried snow shovels.

Howie shuddered. "Besides, it won't be nice when Mr. Mason stomps us into little bitty bits of bite-sized kid pellets."

Liza giggled. "Mr. Mason may be a

grouch, but I don't really think he'd eat a kid for lunch."

"No," Eddie said, "he'd probably save us for dinner."

"Get a grip on yourself," Melody told him as they stepped into Mr. Mason's yard. "Mr. Mason is a man, not a man-eating tiger."

"If Mr. Mason is a man, then why does he growl so much?" Eddie said.

Melody opened her mouth to answer, but a loud roar stopped her.

Liza whimpered and held up her snow shovel like a machine gun. "W–what was that?" she asked.

Howie shook his head. "It sure sounded like a tiger to me."

The roar got louder. Liza dropped her shovel and covered her ears. Eddie's knees started shaking and Howie dropped his plate of cookies.

"Hey," the roaring voice yelled. "I told you to stay off my property!" Mr. Mason

stood inside the opened door and shook his fist at them.

"Oh, my gosh," Liza squealed. "He's going to beat us up."

"Don't be silly," Melody told her. "My guardian angel wouldn't let that happen." Melody walked right up to Mr. Mason's porch and smiled.

"My name is Melody," she told him. "I brought you some Christmas cookies. And my friends and I are going to shovel the snow off your sidewalks for you."

"We'll decorate your yard for Christmas, too," Liza said.

"We want to be your friends," Howie added.

Mr. Mason scowled and leaned toward Melody. He grabbed a cookie shaped like a star. He popped the whole cookie in his mouth. Then he reached out and snatched the plate right from Melody's hands.

12

A New Guard

Eddie tried to catch a fat snowflake on his tongue while Howie and Melody waited for Liza to catch up. It was early Wednesday morning and they were on their way to school.

"I can't believe we spent the entire evening decorating Mr. Mason's yard," Eddie complained as soon as Liza joined her friends. "And all he did was eat cookies."

Howie nodded. "He didn't even share."

Melody smiled and kept walking down the sidewalk. They were almost at the corner when she said, "We didn't bring the cookies for ourselves."

"I think it's nice that we decorated his whole yard," Liza said.

"And I'll think it's nice when you decorate *my* yard," Eddie snapped.

Melody started to say something, but her words were cut short by the crossing guard's shrill whistle. But it wasn't Miss Michaels' whistle.

Mr. Mason blew the whistle again and motioned for the kids to cross the street. "Good morning, kids!"

"It'd be a better morning if we didn't have to go to school," Eddie grumbled.

"When did you become the crossing guard?" Howie asked.

Melody stomped the snow off her boots and said, "What happened to Angela Michaels?"

"One question at a time." Mr. Mason laughed. "Miss Michaels thought I would enjoy this job. She was right. Unfortunately, that delightful creature had to fly off on some important business."

"What about the karate school?" Eddie asked. "I was just learning a sidekick."

Mr. Mason smiled. "There are other teachers. Miss Michaels was just here for the opening. I will certainly miss her."

Liza patted Mr. Mason on the back. "Don't worry," she said. "We're your friends now. You won't ever be lonely again."

"Come on, Miss Goody Two-shoes," Eddie said, pulling on Liza's arm. "Let's get to school."

The four kids walked up the school driveway. Liza looked back at Mr. Mason and waved. "I never would have believed he'd be so nice," she said. "I'm glad we became friends."

"It was all because of Melody's sugar cookies," Howie said. "He ate the whole plate by himself."

"I guess he doesn't get many home-made cookies," Melody said.

Liza giggled. "I thought he was going to squish you and all he did was grab the cookies."

"My guardian angel protected me," Melody told them.

"Oh, no." Eddie stumbled around the driveway pretending to be sick. "Melody's gone nuts again."

"Didn't you hear Mr. Mason tell us that Angela Michaels flew away?" Melody said. "*Flew* as in angels."

"I can fly on a plane, too," Howie reminded her.

"You never proved that Angela Michaels was an angel," Eddie said, crossing his arms over his chest.

Melody looked up at the sky and smiled. "Some things you don't have to prove," she said. "Some things you just believe in . . . like angels!"

The Adventures of THE BAILEY SCHOOL KIDS

The owner of the new Jewel's Pizza Castle is dressed up like a knight. The sign over the kitchen door says "The Dungeon." Could the cook really be a fire-breathing *dragon*?

It's up to Howie and the rest of The Bailey School Kids to find out the secret to the best-tasting pizza in town!

The Adventures of The Bailey School Kids #24

Dragons Don't Cook Pizza

by Debbie Dadey and Marcia Thornton Jones

Creepy, weird, wacky and funny things happen to the Bailey School Kids!™ Collect and read them all!

The Adventures of THE BAILEY SCHOOL KIDS®